WHEN I AM ANGRY

written by Michael Gordon

illustrated by Max Larin

THIS BOOK BELONGS TO

....

....

AGE: ....

As you may or may not know, it's not fun feeling mad.
It's even worse when you're angry with your mom or your dad.
So, when anger comes around and wants to ruin your day,
Get rid of it fast so you can continue to play.

For the most part, Josh was sweet and as fun as can be.
Except when he lost his temper, which was often, you see.
Today's angry mood started just after morning play.
Josh wanted cake before lunch but his mom said, "NO WAY!"

Josh started to breathe heavily, his heart beating fast.
He gritted his teeth and hoped the feelings wouldn't last.
Mom taught Josh a trick to stop anger from ruining his day.
"Pretend anger is a ball and throw that ball far away."

Josh threw three big balls of anger as far as he could.
Before long, it was all gone and Josh was feeling good.
He sat down and ate lunch and had cake when he was done.
Mom was proud that Josh had battled his anger and won.

When Josh was at the park with his sister later that day,
They saw a black and white cat that Mom said was a stray.
Josh wanted to keep the cat and take it home with them all.
When Mom said, "No," Josh got angry. He threw an anger ball.

Although it made him feel better, he was still really mad.
So, his sister suggested a trick she'd learned from their dad.
"Dad said when you feel so angry that you just want to shout,
Take a deep breath, count to four, and then let it all out."

This worked well for Josh.
Soon, he was back to enjoying his day.

Until he was in the front yard later, trying to play.

Some big boys were heading to the park to play in the sun.

Josh wanted to go with them, he thought it would be fun.

Dad said Josh wasn't big enough to leave his parents' sight.
Josh felt angry. He clenched his fists and his chest felt tight.
He tried all the tricks but couldn't manage it alone.
So, Dad breathed with him until he could do it on his own.

The next day, while out shopping, Josh wanted a new toy.

When Mom said, "Not today," he became an angry little boy.

He yelled, cried, kicked, and stomped; he
made a huge scene in the store.

Mom took him out quickly and sat him down on the floor.

They took lots of deep breaths and made balls of anger to throw.
Josh threw a lot of balls before his anger started to go.
"It's fine to be angry," Mom said, "but don't let it ruin your day.
I'm proud of how you've calmed down by sending anger away."

Your opinion could change the world!

I hope you enjoyed this little story. Reviews from awesome customers like you help other parents to feel confident about choosing this book too.

Would you mind taking a minute to leave your feedback?

I will be forever grateful!

Michael

Thank you!

★★★★★

About author

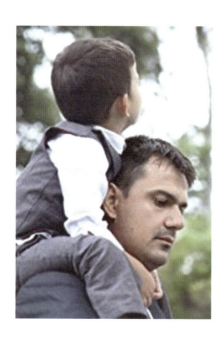

Michael Gordon is the talented author of several highly rated children's books including the popular Sleep Tight, Little Monster, and the Animal Bedtime.

He collaborates with the renowned Kids Book Book that creates picture books for all of ages to enjoy. Michael's goal is to create books that are engaging, funny, and inspirational for children of all ages and their parents.

Contact

For all other questions about books or author,
please e-mail michaelgordonclub@gmail.com.

Self-Regulation Skills (7 book series)

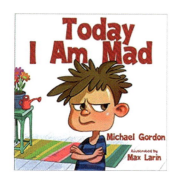

Today I Am Mad

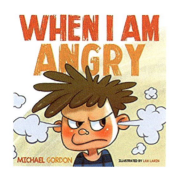

When I am Angry

When I Feel Frustrated

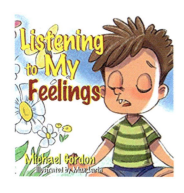

Listening to My Feelings

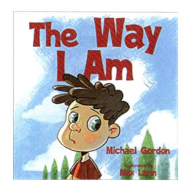

The Way I Am

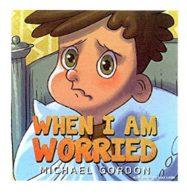

When I Am Worried

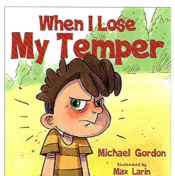

When I Lose My Temper

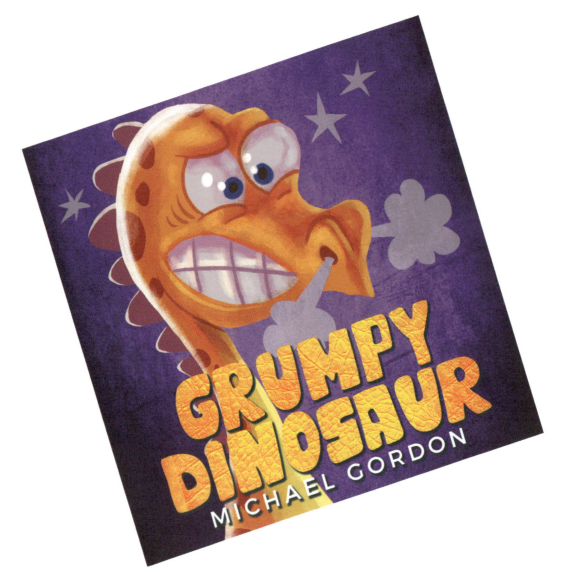

Go https://michaelgordonclub.wixsite.com/books
to get "The Grumpy Dinosaur"
for **FREE!**

Printed in Great Britain
by Amazon